Pet Friends Forever
The Doggone Dog

by Diana G. Gallagher
illustrated by Adriana Isabel Juárez Puglisi

Raintree is an imprint of Capstone Global Library Limited,
a company incorporated in England and Wales having its registered office at 7 Pilgrim
Street, London, EC4V 6LB – Registered company number: 6695582

www.raintreepublishers.co.uk
myorders@raintreepublishers.co.uk

Edited by Helen Cox Cannons
Designed by Kristi Carlson and Philippa Jenkins
Original illustrations © Capstone Global Library Ltd 2014
Image Credits: Shutterstock/Kudryashka (pattern)

Originated by Capstone Global Library Ltd
Production by Helen McCreath
Printed and bound in China

ISBN 978 1 406 27965 8
18 17 16 15 14
10 9 8 7 6 5 4 3 2 1

British Library Cataloguing in Publication Data
A full catalogue record for this book is available from the British Library.

TABLE OF CONTENTS

The park disaster

As he did most afternoons after school, Kyle Blake headed to the local park with his best friend and next-door neighbour, Mia Perez, and Rex, his yellow Labrador retriever.

The park was the perfect place to play fetch with Rex. The yellow Lab needed plenty of exercise, or else he tended to get into trouble around the house.

Mia sat on a bench nearby, watching as Kyle played with his dog. The park was crowded today, especially since a dog obedience class was taking place there.

Kyle held up a stick. "Ready, boy?" he called.

Rex barked, then jumped and turned in excited circles as he waited for Kyle to throw the stick.

Mia looked over from her spot on the bench and watched Rex spin around. "You'd better throw it before he gets dizzy and falls over!" she called.

Kyle tossed the stick across the park. "Get it, boy!" he yelled.

Rex didn't have to be told twice. He took off running across the park. But Kyle's aim wasn't as good as he'd thought. The stick sailed through the air and headed right for the dog obedience class.

"Look out!" Mia yelled. But the class was too far away to hear her warning. The stick landed smack dab in the middle of the circle.

Rex leapt over a cocker spaniel and picked up the stick. He stood still for a moment, looking around. It almost seemed like he was waiting for someone to notice what a good job he'd done fetching the stick.

All the dogs in the obedience class noticed. They immediately started pulling on their leashes and barking at the intruder.

"Quiet, Percy!" a man scolded his little Chihuahua. The dog bounced on all fours and kept yapping.

"No, Winston!" one of the women yelled as her German shepherd dragged her across the park.

The whole time, Rex sat calmly in the middle of the circle, still holding the stick proudly in his mouth.

The trainer moved from dog to dog, trying to calm them down. It seemed to be working until Rex suddenly took off. He ran between two dogs and leapt back out of the circle. The dogs immediately started barking all over again.

"Sorry!" Kyle yelled to the instructor.

Rex trotted over and proudly dropped the stick at Kyle's feet. The trainer shook his head and scowled at them.

Kyle scratched Rex behind the ears. It wasn't like he'd broken the rules – he wasn't even in the class! "All those dogs should fail obedience class," he said.

Rex just panted and thumped his tail on the ground. As long as Kyle was petting, feeding or playing with him, he was happy.

"No more catch today," Kyle said as he walked towards Mia. "I don't think the other dogs could take it."

Rex flopped on the ground and rested his chin on his paws. He looked up at Kyle with sad, pleading eyes.

"I think Rex still wants to play," Mia said when Kyle sat down next to her. "He's not ready for fetch to be over."

"He'll forget about sticks the minute he sees a squirrel," Kyle said. He laughed when Rex jumped up less than a minute later. "See?"

Rex chased a speedy squirrel up a tree. He barked when it disappeared in the leaves. Then he sat down to wait for the squirrel to come back.

"That should keep him busy for a while," Kyle said. "Did you start working on your project for science class yet?"

Mia shook her head. "No," she said. "Do you want to come over after this and work on it together?"

Kyle nodded. "Okay," he agreed. "I need help deciding what I'm going to do. Maybe we'll have better luck coming up with something together."

"Good idea," Mia said. She suddenly glanced around the park. "Hey, where did Rex go?"

Kyle looked over at the tree, but Rex wasn't there. He couldn't believe it. He'd only looked away for a second.

Kyle looked around the park frantically, but didn't see his dog anywhere. Rex was missing!

Rex finds a friend

"Oh, no!" Kyle said. He jumped up and scanned the nearby area. "Where could he have gone?"

"There he is!" Mia said, pointing to the other side of the park.

Kyle sighed with relief when he saw Rex trotting towards him. But the dog wasn't alone. A small, scruffy-looking brown dog was following along behind him.

"Who's your friend, Rex?" Mia asked, scratching the new arrival behind his ears. His ears flopped a little over as Mia petted him.

Rex sat down. The new dog sat down next to him and wagged his stubby tail.

"He doesn't have a collar," Mia said. "Do you think he's a stray?"

"I don't know," Kyle said. "Maybe he just slipped out and got away."

"Maybe," Mia said. "Let's wait here. His owner could be in the park."

Mia and Kyle played with Rex and his new friend for almost thirty minutes, hoping someone would come looking for a lost dog and see them. But no one did.

"I bet his owner doesn't know he's gone," Mia said.

"I bet you're right," Kyle said. "We don't even know where the dog came from. We should look for his owner."

"Good idea!" Mia said, standing up.

Kyle snapped his leash on Rex's collar, but then he paused. "We don't have a leash for the other dog," he said. "What if he runs away from us? "

"I don't think that's a problem," Mia said as they started walking with Rex. The little dog trotted quickly to keep up with his new friend. When Kyle and Rex stopped, the little dog stopped, too. Mia smiled. "See what I mean? It seems like he'll go wherever Rex goes."

Most people in the park had their dogs with them. But Kyle and Mia spotted an old man sitting on a bench towards the outside of the park, away from the action. He was reading a newspaper.

"Maybe it's that man's dog," Mia suggested. "And he didn't notice that it wandered off because he's reading. I mean, Rex wandered off on us, and we were just talking."

"Excuse me, sir," Kyle said as they walked over. "Is this your dog?"

The man lowered his newspaper and frowned. "No," he said. "I don't like dogs."

Mia frowned. "Then why are you at the park?" she asked.

"Everybody is too busy with their dogs to sit down," the old man said. "There's always an empty bench. That's why."

With that, the old man put the paper in front of his face again and went back to reading.

Taking the hint, Kyle and Mia moved on. Just outside the dog park they saw two boys playing football. Kyle didn't see a dog anywhere near them.

"Hey!" Kyle called over to them.

Both boys looked over. "What?" the taller one asked.

"Is this your dog?" Mia asked, patting the lost dog's head.

The boy shook his head and made a face. "Who'd want a scruffy-looking mutt like that?" he asked.

"Not me!" his friend agreed, shaking his head and laughing.

Kyle and Mia exchanged a look and kept walking. "I think you're cute, Scruffy," Mia told the lost dog.

They kept walking, all the way around the entire park. As they neared the entrance, they spotted a woman and a little girl. The woman looked upset, and the little girl was crying.

"I bet the dog belongs to them," Kyle said. "She's probably upset she can't find it."

Kyle and Mia walked over, but when they got closer, the little girl pointed at Rex and screamed. Kyle and Mia came to a stop.

"Sorry," the woman said. "Callie is afraid of dogs. I thought showing her how much fun people have with them might help, but it clearly didn't."

Kyle and Mia nodded and quickly walked away with the two dogs. There was obviously no point in asking the woman if the scruffy dog belonged to them.

"We've asked every dogless person here," Mia said. "Now what?"

"Well, we can't just leave him here," Kyle said. "He needs food and water and a place to sleep. Besides, he has to belong to someone."

"I'd bring him home with me, but Misty wouldn't like it," Mia said.

Kyle nodded. Mia's cat didn't seem to like anything, especially dogs. Misty had scratched Rex's nose – twice! Luckily, Kyle's mum was a vet, so she had quickly cleaned up the little scratch.

"Then Scruffy will have to go home with me," Kyle said. "He and Rex obviously get along. Maybe my mum will know what to do."

Scruffy gets a break

When Kyle and Mia got to his house, his mum was still working. Luckily, Dr Blake's veterinary clinic was right next to Kyle's house, so they headed next door to talk to her about the dog they'd found.

Lillian, Dr Blake's receptionist, was seated at the front desk when they walked in. "Hello, what are you up to?" she greeted them as they walked in.

Just then, she noticed Scruffy standing by Kyle's side. "Who's this?" she asked.

"We found him in the park," Mia explained.

"Is my mum around?" Kyle asked. "We need to talk to her for a minute."

"Sure, go on back," Lillian said. "She just finished up with her last patient, so she should be in her office."

"Thanks, Lillian!" Mia said.

Kyle and Mia headed down a hallway with exam rooms on both sides and turned a corner. Dr Blake's office was at the back of the clinic.

Kyle stuck his head into the office. "Hi, Mum," he said. "Do you have a second?"

"Of course," his mum said. "I always have time for you. What's up?"

"Well, I have a problem," Kyle said. "But it's just temporary."

Mia stepped into the room, holding the little dog in her arms. "He's lost," she said. "We found him at the park."

"Well, technically Rex found him," Kyle said. "And then he found us. We asked everyone, but Scruffy didn't belong to anyone in the park."

Dr Blake arched an eyebrow. "Scruffy?" she asked.

"I had to call him something," Kyle explained.

"Just until we find out what his real name is," Mia said. "And where he lives."

"We should take him to the pet rescue centre," Dr Blake said. "That's the best place to take a lost dog. People who lose pets usually call there first."

"But he might get sick there," Kyle argued.

"No, he won't," Dr Blake said. "They don't put healthy animals and sick ones in the same area."

"The big dogs might pick on him," Mia said.

"Yeah," Kyle agreed. "Can't he stay here? Just for a little while. Mia and I want to find his owner."

"Please," Mia pleaded.

Rex barked, and the little dog put his front paws on Dr Blake's arm. He looked at her with sad eyes and whined.

"All right, I give up!" Dr Blake said with a laugh. "But just for the weekend."

"Thanks, Mum!" Kyle said, grinning happily.

"I'll have to give him a quick exam," Dr Blake said. "I can't risk him getting any of the other animals sick."

There were lots of other dogs and cats in the clinic. Some were sick, and some were recovering from surgery. Others were just being boarded there while their owners were on holiday.

Before they took Scruffy to a cage, Dr Blake listened to his heart and checked his ears. Then she checked for worms.

"I don't see anything, but I don't know what shots he's had. I'll put him in a cage away from the other animals, just in case," Dr Blake said.

Scruffy didn't like it when they closed him in a roomy cage. He turned around and around in circles and pawed at the bars. He barked, whined and howled.

"Maybe he'll settle down if we leave," Dr Blake suggested.

They all went back to Dr Blake's office, but it was no use. A few minutes later, Scruffy was still barking.

"Well, he can't stay in here," Dr Blake said. "All that noise will upset the patients that have to stay overnight."

"He can stay in my room with Rex," Kyle offered quickly. "We already know he and Rex get along, and tomorrow is Saturday. Mia and I can spend the whole day trying to find his home."

"And Sunday, too," Mia said.

Dr Blake frowned, but then she sighed. "Okay," she said, "but just until Monday. If we haven't found his owner by then we'll have to call the pet rescue centre."

Nobody's dog

Scruffy calmed down as soon as they moved him into Kyle's room with Rex. He didn't bark or act up, and he slept all night. The next morning, he sat quietly while Kyle poured dog food into two separate bowls.

Rex gobbled his up in seconds, but Scruffy didn't eat much. Instead, he stretched out on the floor with his head on his paws and stared at his dish.

"You miss your owner, don't you, boy?" Kyle asked. Scruffy wagged his stubby tail as if to say yes.

After he'd finished eating, Rex ran to the back door and waited to be let outside. Kyle grabbed a tennis ball and took both dogs outside to play.

Mia walked over from her house just as they started playing fetch. Scruffy seemed to like chasing the tennis ball as much as Rex did.

"How did Scruffy do last night in your room?" Mia asked.

"He was okay," Kyle said. "He didn't bark or cry, so that was good. But he barely ate anything this morning. I think he misses his owner."

"Maybe we should look online and see if anyone has posted an ad for a missing dog," Mia suggested. "I think the newspaper posts lost pet ads for free."

"Good idea!" Kyle said.

He and Mia brought Scruffy and Rex back in the house and headed to Kyle's room to use the computer. They read through every single missing-dog ad on the newspaper's website, but nobody was looking for a little dog that looked like Scruffy.

"Maybe it's too soon," Kyle said. "Scruffy's owner might have waited to see if he came home last night. And then it would have been too late to post an ad."

"You could be right," Mia said. "Let's take the dogs for a walk. Maybe someone put up flyers for a missing dog."

"Great idea!" Kyle said. "If Rex was missing, I'd post flyers everywhere. Even if it took all night."

Kyle and Mia grabbed an extra collar and leash for Scruffy from the clinic next door. Kyle's mum always had spares around, just in case.

Scruffy didn't seem to mind wearing a collar. He didn't try to pull ahead when they headed down the pavement.

"He's so well behaved," Mia said as they walked. "That must mean he has an owner somewhere."

They walked a few streets over to the park where they'd found Scruffy the day before. There were no flyers posted on the bulletin board in the park.

Then they walked all around the neighbourhood, but no one had posted a sign for a missing dog.

Kyle's mum was drinking coffee in the kitchen when they got home. Her clinic was only open until noon on Saturdays.

"No luck?" Dr Blake asked when they walked in.

Mia shook her head sadly. "Maybe somebody called the pet rescue centre, like you said," she suggested.

"Can you find out?" Kyle asked. His mum knew everyone in town who had anything to do with animals.

"Of course," Dr Blake said. She dialled the number for the pet rescue centre. She spoke to one of the volunteers and described Scruffy.

But when she hung up, Kyle could tell she didn't have good news.

Dr Blake shook her head. "Sorry," she said. "Nobody came in looking for a dog matching Scruffy's description."

"Well, I'm not giving up," Kyle said. He leaned over and picked up Scruffy. "There could be a reason his owner didn't post an ad or put up flyers. What if they don't have a computer or a printer?"

"There has to be something else can we do," Mia said.

"Maybe we could put up flyers," Kyle suggested.

"Good idea!" Mia agreed. "We can put them up around the neighbourhood and in the park."

Mia and Kyle headed to his room, and got right to work. They took pictures of Scruffy and uploaded them to the computer. Then they put a caption beneath the photo that said, "Small dog found in park on Friday afternoon." They added the phone number for Kyle's house and printed out several copies.

"That should do it," Kyle said, taking the papers out of the printer.

When he turned around, Kyle gasped. They'd been so busy working on the flyers that they hadn't been paying much attention to the dogs. Rex was asleep on the floor, but Scruffy was chewing on a T-shirt that Kyle had left out.

"Oh, no!" Kyle exclaimed. He grabbed the shirt out of Scruffy's mouth and examined it. There was a big hole right in the middle.

Mia grimaced. "He probably did it because he's nervous," she said. "I bet he just wants to go home."

"No matter why he did it, my mum is not going to be happy," Kyle said. He hid the torn shirt in one of his dresser drawers. "I'll tell her about it – but not until after we find Scruffy's owner."

"Good plan," Mia said. "Maybe we should take the dogs next door to the clinic while we hang the flyers. That way Scruffy won't be able to get into any more trouble in here while we're gone."

Then they took the flyers, a hammer and some tacks and went for another long walk around the neighbourhood. They posted a flyer on every corner.

"There," Mia said. "Now anybody who lives within ten blocks of the park will see one of the signs. We'll definitely find Scruffy's owner."

"I sure hope so," Kyle said, looking worried. "Otherwise we're going to have to take him to the pet rescue centre in two days."

Too much trouble

The next morning, Mia came over to Kyle's house bright and early.

"Did you get any calls about the flyers last night?" she asked as soon as she arrived. "Do we know where Scruffy came from yet?"

"No," Kyle said, shaking his head. "I guess Scruffy's owner didn't see any of them. I was sure those flyers would do the trick."

"Maybe we should check online again," Mia suggested. "Someone could have posted an ad last night when Scruffy didn't come home."

"Good plan," Kyle said. But before they could do anything, a loud crash sounded in the kitchen.

"Kyle!" his mum shouted. "Come in here right now!"

Kyle and Mia exchanged a look. That didn't sound good. They raced to the kitchen.

When they got there, it was easy to see why Kyle's mum was so upset. Food wrappers, boxes, crumpled paper and other rubbish were scattered all across the kitchen floor. The rubbish bin had been knocked over and lay on its side with rubbish spilling out.

In the opposite corner of the kitchen, Rex and Scruffy sat near the counter looking extremely guilty.

"I came back from the clinic to get something, and this is the mess I found," his mum said.

Kyle cringed. He knew right away what had happened. Knocking over the rubbish bin was one of Rex's favourite things to do. Apparently having a partner in crime made it even better.

"Bad dogs!" Kyle scolded them. "Rubbish is not for playing with!"

Rex hung his head and looked ashamed, but Scruffy just wagged his tail happily. Apparently he didn't agree with Kyle's feelings about rubbish.

"I have to get back over to the clinic," Kyle's mum said. "Clean up the mess and put the dogs outside."

Kyle nodded. Picking up the rubbish was gross, but the dogs were his responsibility. "I'll do it right now," he said.

"I'll help you," Mia offered.

Mia put Rex and Scruffy out in the garden. Rex immediately went off looking for squirrels. For once, Scruffy didn't follow him. Instead, he sat next to the backdoor and watched as they cleaned up the mess.

Mia swept up coffee grounds and orange peels. Kyle gathered the paper towels and food wrappers back into the rubbish bag and tied it shut.

When the kitchen was clean, Mia and Kyle headed to Kyle's room to look for missing-dog ads online. Scruffy started barking as soon as they left the room.

"So do you think we should go and get him?" Mia asked.

"I'm sure he'll be fine," Kyle said. "Rex is out there to play with him, and the gate is closed. It'll be harder for him to get in trouble out there than in the house."

"Good point," Mia said.

The children got to work searching online. There were two new ads for lost dogs on the newspaper website, but Scruffy wasn't a beagle or a golden retriever.

The whole time they looked, Scruffy was barking outside.

"Kyle!" his mum finally shouted. "Can you please make that dog be quiet? I can hear him all the way next door. He's driving the other animals mad."

"Coming!" Kyle called. He and Mia hurried back downstairs. Scruffy stopped barking just before they reached the kitchen.

"Rex probably got tired of waiting for squirrels and decided to play," Mia said.

Kyle looked at the clock. "It's almost 11 o'clock, and no one has called about Scruffy yet," he said. "I'm getting worried. What if Scruffy's owner isn't even looking for him?"

"That can't be true," Mia said, shaking her head. "Everyone at the park thought Scruffy was adorable."

"Except for those two guys playing football," Kyle reminded her.

"They don't count," Mia said. "If we don't find Scruffy's old home, I'm sure we can find him a new one. Let's go play outside with the dogs for a while."

"Do you mind listening for the phone while we're outside?" Kyle asked his mum. "I don't want to miss Scruffy's owner calling."

"Of course," his mum agreed. "I'll let you know if anyone calls."

"Thanks, Mum," Kyle said.

"I don't think Scruffy gets the point of fetch," Kyle told Mia as they headed for the back door. "He likes to chase the ball, but he doesn't like to bring it back. He wants me to chase him!"

Mia laughed. "Maybe he's teaching you to play chase," she suggested.

But when they got outside and looked around, they both stopped laughing. Scruffy hadn't stopped barking because he and Rex were playing.

He'd stopped barking because he was gone.

Pound or found?

"Scruffy!" Kyle yelled as he frantically looked around the back garden. Rex was sitting by the gate that led to the front garden. But Scruffy was nowhere to be seen.

"Scruffy, where are you?" Mia called, looking behind bushes and the garden shed. "Come here, boy!"

Then Kyle noticed the big hole beneath the gate leading out of the garden.

"Oh, no! Look!" Kyle exclaimed. "He must have got out. What if his owner calls now, and he's lost again?"

Just then, Kyle's mum came out into the back garden. "What's all the yelling about, Kyle?" she asked.

"Scruffy dug a hole under the gate and escaped," Mia explained.

"We have to go and look for him straight away," Kyle said. He hurried over to the back door and grabbed Rex's leash off a hook.

"If you don't find him in a few minutes, come back," his mum said. "Lillian can watch the clinic for a few minutes while I drive you around the neighbourhood. We'll cover more ground that way."

"Thanks, Mum," Kyle said. He snapped the leash onto Rex's collar and opened the gate. He left it open just in case Scruffy wanted to sneak back in.

"He probably didn't get very far," Mia said as they hurried towards the front garden.

"I hope not," Kyle replied. He felt really awful. Scruffy was his responsibility for the time being. He didn't want anything bad to happen to him.

When they got to the front garden, Rex started barking. He jumped forward, pulling the leash out of Kyle's hand. He ran straight to the front porch and started digging in the flowers near the front steps. He never, ever did that – unless he was looking for a buried bone.

"Did you find Scruffy, Rex?" Kyle asked hopefully.

Mia stooped down to look in the bushes. "He certainly did," she said. "And the bone Scruffy stole."

She reached into the bushes and pulled Scruffy out by the collar.

Kyle let out a sigh of relief. They took the dogs back into the back garden and locked the gate behind them. Then they used dirt to fill in the hole Scruffy had dug and took both dogs inside.

As they came in the back door, Kyle's mum walked into the house through the door that connected it to her clinic. "How's it going?" she asked.

"Great!" Kyle said quickly. "Just perfect."
He didn't want his mum to know how much
trouble Scruffy was getting into. He knew she
might make them call the pet rescue centre a
day early.

"Yeah," Mia added. "Totally perfect. No
problems at all."

"Really?" his mum said. She gave Kyle and
Mia a knowing look. "You mean besides all the
barking and playing in the trash and digging
out of the back garden? Other than that he's
been totally perfect?"

"Um . . ." Kyle started to say.

"And you haven't got any calls from his
owner yet," his mum continued. "Is that about
right?"

Kyle sighed. "Pretty much," he admitted unhappily.

"So it sounds like we have a bit of a problem," his mum said. "Scruffy is too noisy to stay in the clinic while you're at school tomorrow, and he's too much trouble to leave in the house alone."

Kyle made a face. Now probably wasn't a good time to tell his mum about the T-shirt Scruffy had wrecked.

"Does that mean Scruffy has to go to the pet rescue centre?" Mia asked.

"I still think that's the best plan," Dr Blake said. "But if I can find someone to watch him during the day, I'll give you two one more day to find his owner."

Just then, the house phone rang. "Hello?" Kyle's mum answered. She paused, and then said, "Yes, that's right we did. Can you describe him?"

Kyle tensed. His mum looked over at Scruffy and nodded.

"Yes, that sounds like the dog my son found," Dr Blake said. She wrote something on the pad of paper next to the phone. "We'll bring him right over."

"Was that Scruffy's owner? Are you absolutely sure it's his dog?" Kyle asked as soon as his mum had put the phone down.

"How come Scruffy ran away in the first place?" Mia asked, frowning.

"Any why didn't his owner put up flyers or an ad or call the pet rescue centre about him?" Kyle added.

"What if Scruffy's home isn't a very good one?" Mia asked. "What if that's why his owner didn't look for him?"

Dr Blake held up her hands to signal them to be quiet. "Slow down," she said. "Yes, I'm sure it's his dog. He described Scruffy exactly. And I'm sure there are good reasons for everything else. Let's go and see."

An old man's story

Kyle and Mia collected Scruffy, and Kyle's mum drove them to the address Scruffy's owner had given her. The house was only a few streets away from the park.

When they pulled up to the house, an elderly man was sitting on a swing on the front porch waiting for them. Scruffy bolted out of the car the instant Kyle opened the passenger-side door.

"Scruffy!" Kyle yelled after him.

"Wait!" Mia shouted, running after the little dog.

But Scruffy didn't listen. Instead, he ran right up to the porch and headed straight for his owner. He leaped onto the old man's lap. Straight away, the little dog started happily licking his owner's face.

"Hey, boy!" the man said with a laugh. "I was so worried. You're lucky these nice people found you."

"We're very happy we found you," Kyle's mum said. He held out his hand. "You must be Mr McCarthy. I'm Kyle's mum, Dr Blake. We spoke on the phone."

"I hope Sam wasn't too much work," Mr McCarthy said. "He gets into a lot of trouble."

"He was fine," Kyle's mum said. "A little barking and some bin-emptying, but we're used to that with our dog."

"Would you three like to come inside and have some lemonade?" Mr McCarthy offered. "I'm parched. Besides, it's the least I can do to thank you for bringing Sam back to me safe and sound."

"Oh, we don't want to bother you," Dr Blake said.

"Don't be silly. It's no bother at all," Mr McCarthy said. "I don't get much company these days."

Mr McCarthy reached for the cane leaning against the porch swing. He stood up very carefully and shuffled slowly towards the door.

Now Kyle knew why Mr McCarthy hadn't put up flyers around the neighbourhood when Scruffy had gone missing. He couldn't. He had trouble walking. He had trouble just making it to his front door.

Inside, Kyle's mum helped Mr McCarthy pour lemonade. Then Kyle and Mia carried the drinks to the backyard.

The first thing Kyle noticed was that Mr McCarthy didn't have a fence. Instead, there was a stake in the ground with a long yard leash attached. A dog collar was still clipped to the end of the leash.

"That must be where Scruffy was when he escaped," he whispered to Mia.

"How did Scruffy – I mean, Sam – get away?" Mia asked Mr McCarthy.

The old man sighed. "My arthritis has got so bad that I haven't been able to play with Sam or take him for walks," he said. "He must have got bored, slipped out of his collar, and gone to have some fun on his own."

Kyle walked over and put the collar back around the dog's neck. He double checked that it was tight.

"I called the pet rescue centre, but they said I had to come in," Mr McCarthy continued. "Most of my friends are elderly, and I couldn't find someone to drive me."

"Well, he's back safe and sound." Kyle scratched Sam behind the ears. The dog licked his hand happily.

"Yes, and I'm very grateful," Mr McCarthy said. Then he sighed. "But I'm worried that sooner or later he'll get bored and take off again. And maybe next time he won't find someone as nice as you two to help him get home."

8

Worry won't solve anything

"I'm worried about Scruffy," Kyle said to Mia at school the next morning.

"I know," Mia said. "Me, too."

"What if he gets away again and doesn't get home the next time?" Kyle said.

Mia shook her head. "Mr McCarthy will be so sad," she said.

Kyle nodded. "So will I," he said.

Their friend Lucy Owens leaned over from her desk. "What are you guys talking about?" she asked.

"Mia and I rescued a dog this weekend," Mia said.

"You got another dog?" Lucy asked, looking surprised. "Isn't Rex jealous?"

"I didn't adopt a dog," Kyle explained. "We found a lost dog in the park."

"And for a little guy, he was a lot of trouble," Mia said. "He and Rex knocked over the rubbish bin, and he wouldn't stop barking. And then he dug a hole under the gate in Kyle's back garden and escaped."

"Don't forget about the hole he chewed in my T-shirt," Kyle added.

"Was your mum mad?" Lucy asked.

"She probably will be . . ." Kyle said slowly. "I haven't exactly told her about that part yet."

"Is he still at your house?" Lucy asked.

Kyle shook his head. "No, we finally found out where he lives," he said. "We put up flyers all weekend, and his owner finally called yesterday."

"He belongs to a really nice old man," Mia said. "We met his owner yesterday when we took Sam back to his house. But Mr McCarthy is too old to play with the little dog or take him for walks."

"We think that's why he ran away," Kyle said. "He got bored being tied up in the back garden."

"If I had a dog, I'd take it for a walk every day," Lucy said. "My brother has a snake. Nobody bothers him when he takes the Great Gorgon for a walk!"

"How do you take a snake for a walk?" Mia asked.

"Eddie wraps him around his arm," Lucy explained.

"No wonder nobody bothers him," Mia replied. "If I saw a giant snake wrapped around someone's arm I think I'd head in the other direction."

Lucy laughed. "So what are you going to do about the dog?" she asked. "If he gets bored, won't he just run away from home again?"

"That's what we're worried about," Kyle said.

"Hey, I have an idea," Lucy said. "Why don't you two walk him for his owner? That way you will still get to see him and play with him, and Sam won't be so bored that he runs away."

"That's a great idea!" Kyle exclaimed. He paused and frowned. "But I don't know if I'll have time to take care of another dog. I already have Rex."

"I'll help out," Lucy offered. "I really want a dog, but my parents won't let me get one since my brother already has a snake. This way I still get to play with a dog, and it helps Sam's owner out."

"Really?" Kyle said.

"Definitely," Lucy said. "I bet some of the other children who can't have dogs will help, too."

"We could take Rex over to play with Sam when we go," Mia suggested. "That way they can still see each other."

"This just might work!" Kyle said. "I can't wait to tell Mr McCarthy."

9

The Scruffy solution

Kyle and Mia went straight to Dr Blake's clinic after school. They couldn't wait to tell her all about Lucy's brilliant idea.

"That's a great plan," Dr Blake agreed when they'd explained it to her. "Let's call Mr McCarthy and see if he's home. If he's okay with it, you can go over this afternoon and tell him your idea."

Kyle dialled Mr McCarthy's number. "Hi, Mr McCarthy," he said. "It's Kyle Blake. Mia and I were wondering if we could come and visit you this afternoon. We have something to talk to you about."

"Of course!" Mr McCarthy said. "Come on over! Why don't you bring Rex with you so he and Sam can play."

"Okay, see you soon!" Kyle said.

The great idea

Sam started barking as soon as Kyle, Mia and Rex walked up Mr McCarthy's drive. He probably smelled them all the way down the block. Dog noses were a lot better than people noses.

"Well, well!" Mr McCarthy was sitting on the porch with Sam next to him on a leash. "We've got company, Sam!"

Sam barked and pulled until Mr McCarthy let him go. Then he ran right up to Rex and bounced all around the big, yellow Labrador retriever.

"I think he's happy to see your dog," Mr McCarthy said. "He missed his new friend."

"Rex is happy to see him, too!" Kyle said.

"Let's head out to the back garden," the old man said. "There's more room back there for the dogs to play."

On their way through the house, they stopped in the kitchen for lemonade.

Kyle was dying to tell Mr McCarthy about their idea, but he waited until they were settled on the back steps.

Then Mia beat him to it.

"We told all our friends about you and Sam, Mr McCarthy," Mia said. "And we came up with a great idea for how to help you and Sam!"

"I don't understand. Help me how?" Mr McCarthy asked, looking back and forth between Kyle and Mia.

"With Sam!" Kyle exclaimed. "Since you have arthritis and can't take Sam for walks, we thought we could take turns coming here to play with him. A group of our friends offered to help out, too."

"That way Sam won't get bored and run away again," Mia said. "And we'll bring Rex with us so they can still play together."

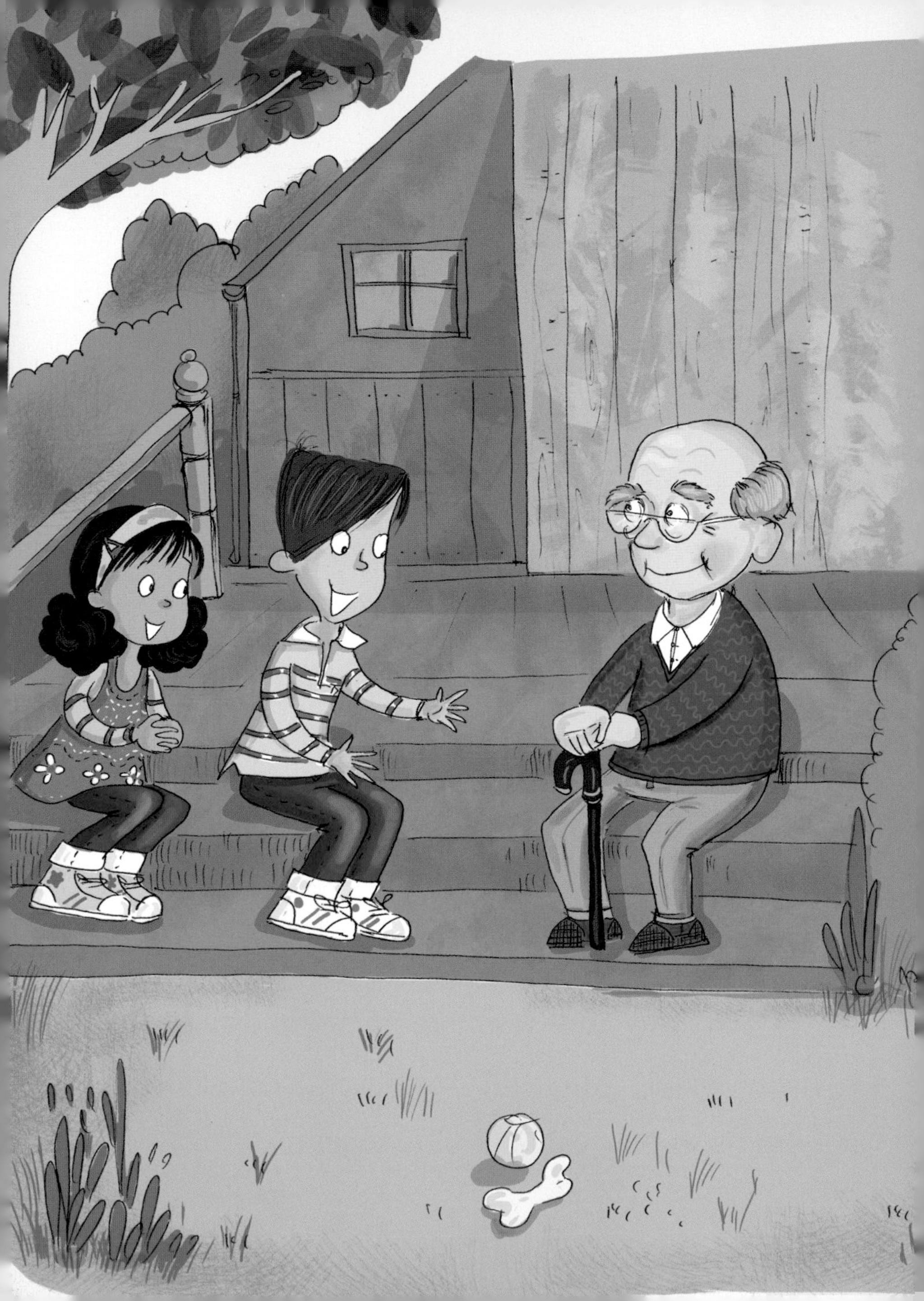

"And our friends who can't have dogs will get a chance to play with one," Kyle finished. "What do you think?"

"I think that's the best idea I've ever heard!" Mr McCarthy said with a smile. "Thank you, both."

They all shook on it. Then, to seal the deal, Kyle and Mia took Rex and Sam to the park to play.

AUTHOR BIO

Diana G. Gallagher lives in Florida, USA, with three dogs, eight cats and a cranky parrot. She has written more than 90 books. When she's not writing, Gallagher likes gardening, garage sales and spending time with her grandchildren.

ILLUSTRATOR BIO

Adriana Isabel Juárez Puglisi has been a freelance illustrator and writer for more than twenty years and loves telling stories. She currently lives in Granada, Spain, with her husband, son, daughter, two dogs, a little bird and several fish.

Glossary

arrival (uh-RYE-vuhl) — someone or something that has got to a particular place

clinic (KLIN-ik) — a place where people can go to receive medical treatment or advice

exercise (EK-sur-size) — physical activity that you do to keep fit and healthy

intruder (in-TROO-dur) — someone who forces their way into a place or situation where they are not wanted or invited

obedience (oh-BEE-dee-uhns) — the act of listening or obeying

relief (ri-LEEF) — a feeling of freedom from pain or worry

CARING FOR YOUR DOG

Dogs can make great pets, but like any animal they also require a lot of work. Want to know more about owning a dog? Here are some quick tips to get you started!

- Dogs need to get plenty of exercise to stay healthy. Taking your dog for walks, running around in the garden and playing fetch are all good ways to keep your dog fit and healthy.

- Your dog should wear a collar and ID tag with your name, address and phone number at all times. This will increase the chances of your dog being returned to you if it gets lost or runs away.

- Your dog's diet depends on its size, age and activity level. Ask your vet to help you find the best food for your dog, and always make sure you provide plenty of fresh, clean water.

- Your dog will need regular check-ups at the doctor, just like you. Make appointments with your veterinarian and don't be afraid to ask questions.

- Bathe your dog on a regular basis. Make sure you use a good shampoo and rinse well. You can also take your dog to a groomer if you need help.

- Dogs never outgrow the need to chew. Having chew toys for your dog to play with will keep your shoes and other things safe.

DISCUSSION QUESTIONS

1. Dogs need lots of exercise. Talk about some different ways owners can help their dogs get exercise.

2. Can you think of any other ways Kyle and Mia could have found the missing dog's owner? Talk about your ideas.

3. Have you ever found something that doesn't belong to you? Talk about what you did to return it to its owner.

WRITING PROMPTS

1. Do you have a pet? What is the hardest part? What is the best part? Write a paragraph about each.

2. Pretend you are Mr McCarthy. Create a flyer or newspaper ad about your missing dog. What information would need to be included?

3. Kyle and Mia decide to go and play with Sam so that he won't run away again. Write a list of some other ways Kyle and Mia could have helped.

Pet Friends Forever

READ THE WHOLE SERIES
and learn more about
Kyle and Mia's animal adventures!

Find them all at
www.raintree.co.uk

Pet Friends Forever
A No-Sneeze Pet
by Diana G. Gallagher

Pet Friends Forever
The Great Kitten Challenge
by Diana G. Gallagher

Pet Friends Forever
Mice Capades
by Diana G. Gallagher

Pet Friends Forever
The Doggone Dog